Lasactka
The End of Human Intelligence

Lasactka
The End of Human Intelligence

Lasactka
The End of Human Intelligence

Lasactka
The End of Human Intelligence

Lasactka
The End of Human Intelligence

Lasactka
The End of Human Intelligence

Lasactka
The End of Human Intelligence

Lena Ma

Copyright © 2020

Lasactka
The End of Human Intelligence

All rights reserved. No part of this publication may be
reproduced, distributed, or transmitted in any form or by any
means, including photocopying, recording, or other electronic
or mechanical methods, without the prior written permission
of the publisher, except in the case of brief quotations
embodied in critical reviews and certain other noncommercial
uses permitted by copyright law.

Any references to historical events, real people, or real places
are used fictitiously. Names, characters, and places are
products of the author's imagination.

Cover Design by Lily Dormishev

Lasactka
The End of Human Intelligence

Lasactka
The End of Human Intelligence

Lasactka
The End of Human Intelligence

Table of Contents

Lasactka
The End of Human Intelligence

Lasactka
The End of Human Intelligence

Chapter One

The Destructive Aftermath

Year 2086

The café is dingy and dark, the overhead lights flickering. Most of the lighting is provided by the blazing sun streaming through the cracks of the windows.

Still, it only aids in highlighting the adhesive spots on the soiled floor.

"Um... I think I did?"

A young woman, dressed in maroon overalls, chestnut brown boots, and a dark grey beret, quietly answers, approaching the counter while violently whacking her phone against the palm of her hand in attempts to get it to turn on.

"Okay, what's your name?" the barista asks the woman. "Um... I forget."

"Miss, are you okay?" the barista probes again.

"I don't know. I think so. Maybe?" The woman blankly stares at a deep groove in the counter, her eyes glazing over. "I'm not quite sure."

"Can I call anyone for you?" The barista eyes the phone the woman is desperately trying to turn on. "Maybe a family member or a friend?"

"I don't remember if I have any." The woman glances around the café. "Where am I?"

"Inside a café, miss. Welcome to Baxxes! Are you sure you're okay?"

"Um... no? Do I like cara... cara... carameeel?" the young woman questions, distracted from their previous conversation.

"I don't know. Do I?" the barista inquires back, unaware of whom the question was directed toward.

"Hmmm... well, if I like it, then you must like it too, right?" the woman confidently answers, taking a sip.

Her eyes widen. "This is the BEST thing I've ever tasted! It tastes like candy! Except, you know, it has water in it. It tastes like candy with water in it! Here, try some!"

She exclaims as she thrusts the cup out toward the barista.

"Really? Candy with water!? No way! I've never heard of such thing before! Give me! Give me! Let me try!"

The enthusiastic barista snatches the cup of caramel macchiato and chugs it.

She hastily spits out the contents within seconds. "HOT!!! IT'S SO HOT!!! AHHHHHH!!!!"

She painfully screams while running her burnt tongue beneath the faucet.

Moments later, the barista turns around and loudly interrogates the young woman. "WHY IS IT SOOOO HOT!?!?!"

The woman, still fascinated and puzzled with getting her phone to turn on, responds, "I think maybe the sun is too hot today so it shines its heat onto the cup, making it hot as well. Maybe it'll be colder tomorrow when the clouds come out. I think it's supposed to rain tomorrow. My dog told me so.

My dog is always right. I love him so much! His name is Mooch, and I would love to show you a picture of him, you know, of him wearing a bumblebee costume last Christmas, but my stupid phone won't turn on. Hey, you have a job! You're smart, right? How do I get this stupid thing to turn on?" The woman forcefully demands as she shoves her phone onto the marble counter in front of the barista.

After minutes of attempting to cool her scorching tongue, the barista takes a look at the young woman's phone. She becomes captivated by the colors of her case as the glitter flowers sparkle beneath the dusty lighting inside the quaint café. She has never seen a contraption this mesmerizing before, and she cannot help but explore every crevice of the phone.

The barista takes her right hand and aggressively strikes the face of the phone a few times, unable to turn it on. She places it under hot water from the faucet since that had loosened her pickle jar earlier, believing the faucet is the answer to everything. Still, no luck.

She then places the phone on the grill, the same grill used to make paninis and flatbreads for the customers, and she attempts to cook the phone on. Nothing.

"Sorry, I think it's broken," the barista shouts as she waves the phone at the young woman.

However, the woman pays no attention to the barista. She is too busy checking out the brooding man across the room, wondering if she could ever look like him. She quickly snaps a picture of him with her disposable camera, throwing it in the trash immediately after as she could never figure out how to get her photos from such a miniscule device.

"Excuse me, ma'am. EXCUSE ME! LISTEN TO ME!" The barista deafeningly repeats. "This is broken. BROKEN!" she squawks as she hands the phone back to the woman.

Without looking up, the young woman waves her hand at the barista. "Oh, just throw it in the trash then. I'll just get another one. All my phones keep breaking. I take a selfie. I lose a phone. I take a selfie. I lose a phone. This keeps happening! Do you know what I mean?"

"Oh yeah, totally!" the barista heartedly agrees. "It happens to me all the time too! That's why I need this job, so I can keep paying for them!"

"I wish there is a button or a key that can just turn on these stupid phones. That would be AMAZING! No, wait! I wish there is a store that sells phones that never break! I should invent one!"

The woman ignorantly declares as she clutches a half-empty iced matcha latte off the table beside her with the name "Logan" written on the side of the cup. "I believe this is mine," she says to the man at the table and walks out.

"Sounds like a fantastic idea! Keep me posted! You can find all my contact information, including my address and credit card number, on my Selfiegram page. I always keep them updated in case anyone needs to find me," the barista bellows behind the woman. "Mocha fra... fra... frapa... frapee... frapee... Who ordered the snow-temperature mocha frapeekeeno!??"

Meanwhile, inside a well-renowned and prestigious medical school...

A cadaver lies open on a steel table. Students are seated behind their desks, copying down a sketch of the human brain from the whiteboard in front of them. Their professor, Dr. Mullesk, paces back and forth, occasionally prodding the corpse with his pencil as he strides.

"Class, who can tell me the mechanism by which a virus latches onto the neural receptors in the brain and prevents the release of the neuron ball-shaped things? Yes, Sarah?" Dr. Mullesk probes.

"Oh, I forget," Sarah responds as she slowly lowers her raised hand.

"Okay, does anyone else know the answer? Yes, Barrett?"

"I'm sorry, what's the question again?" Barrett asks.

"The mechanism of... the mechanism of... of... Hold on, let me look it up again," Dr. Mullesk replies as he rummages through his textbook once more. "Shoot, now I can't find it. Alright, class, you can all go home. NO SCHOOL!"

Across the street from the medical school...

Sirens blare, lights flashing blue and red against the passing cars as a portly police officer walks over to the offender's vehicle. He keeps one hand hovering over his gun as the window of the automobile rolls down.

"Sir, do you know how fast you were going?" the officer interrogates.

"Really, really fast! LIKE A RACE CAR! I want to be a race car driver when I grow up!" the 50-year-old man inside the SUV exclaims.

"Really? Well, then, I think you need to go even faster if you want to win! Good luck!" the police officer cheers on the offender, walking away and letting the man go.

Behind the scene, a woman is holding onto her toddler's hand and begins to cross a busy street...

"Lauren, you are receiving an incoming call from your mother. Do you wish to accept?" the automated voice receptor of the woman's phone announces.

Lauren stops in the middle of the crowded street to answer her phone, unaware that the light has changed and cars are beginning to speed toward her. Her toddler pulls urgently on her skirt, itching to finish crossing, but Lauren pushes the small hand away and pulls her purple velvet skirt back up as she raises her phone to her ear.

"Hello?" Lauren answers. "Yes, this is Lauren. Who is this? Actually, who's Lauren again?"

"Hey! Watch where you're going, you stupid bitch!" one of the drivers screams, heavily drunk, failing to steer away from Lauren and her toddler.

A crackling crunch is heard as the colliding bodies crush against the front of the vehicle. The blunt momentum sends them flying, blood spilling across the pavement.

Glass shatters as the bodies break through the front window of the café. Not a single person inside the café looks up, and instead, continues to sip their cappuccinos as if nothing has happened. The stares of the patrons are slack, and slobber drips from the mouth of one woman sitting by the back door.

Outside, the siren stops blaring. The police officer, becoming one with those inside the café, steps over the limp bodies as he enters Baxxes and sits at a table.

"Hey! Watch where you're flying!" the barista yells as she finds the mess of glass shards and corpses on her floor. "I just cleaned that!"

Blood pours from the flaccid bodies. Person after person enters the picturesque café, stepping over the corpses without saying a word, even as the blood stains their shoes.

The patrons of the café remain silent, carrying on with their daily routines as if nothing unusual around them is happening.

Lasactka
The End of Human Intelligence

Chapter Two

The Infection Begins

Year 2085

"Ladies and gentlemen, welcome to the 50th anniversary of the Synapselligence Awards. As many of you know, the Synapselligence Award is bestowed every year to the scientist who has successfully proven the greatest breakthrough among scientific history. These awards are only presented to the very best, the rare few who have proven their capability and intelligence in changing the face of the Earth.

This year, the Synapselligence Society of Scientific Significance would like to grant the award to Samantha Mare for her groundbreaking creation of 'Lasactka', a novel virus proven to increase the intelligence quotients of all human beings to 200, generating a knowledgeable and civilized society where we can become capable of conquering all feats. Let's welcome Samantha Mare!"

The vast audience of scientists, researchers, professors, and physicians enviously clapped as Samantha gracefully walked onto the stage. She was dressed in a sleek silver gown with matching heels and dangling platinum diamond earrings.

Samantha Mare was a beautiful woman, her skin glowing under the light as her long brown waves brushed through the air. Although physical stunning, Samantha was also intellectual, independent, and resilient, and many scientists found her intimidating.

Her unique mind allowed her to think of unimaginable creations and inventions, causing her colleagues to both praise her and become covetous of her.

She held her head high as she strode among her colleagues. Not a single person in the room had achieved what she had, and none ever would, not without her help at least.

Boldly standing tall, Samantha knew she had changed the face of society. It was time others came to terms with what that really meant. For better or worse, they would all be equals in the truest sense of the word.

"Thank you, Chris. Thank you so much. I'm so honored and grateful to be given this year's Synapselligence Award. The Lasactka virus has been my primary research focus for the past five years, starting from when I worked as a post-doctoral fellow at the underground laboratory of Hygoltz in the heart of the Himalayas with the well-known and loved, Dr. Farrow.

The Lasactka virus is a hydrophilic organism that thrives on the fluids inside our brains. It travels from neuron to neuron via mechanism by the synapses, multiplying, until it spreads out and is collected and released with the neurotransmitters into the rest of our bodies.

Lasactka
The End of Human Intelligence

The Lasactka virus alters the way our bodies interact with our brains, providing us with great strength and balance as our two conflicting parts merge into one being. This physical and mental balance channels our energies within and allows us to reach deep inside ourselves and unleash the knowledge we already possess but fail to use.

We are a society of great potential. However, we only utilize a fraction of our brains throughout our entire lifetimes while failing to see that we are capable of using much more. We allow our insecurities to prevent us from channeling our inner intelligence.

We see others as more intellectual because of their higher IQs, and we hold back while assuming others will carry on the success of our union.

But look around you! Our civilization is deteriorating with each passing day. Technology is crashing. Computers are leaking personal data because our privacy systems have been built with half a brain. Our medical devices are only doing what is 'just enough' to prevent death without seeking to promote greater health, and even then, patients are still dying. Automobiles have been faltering for the past seven years because we still follow blueprints from 30 years ago.

We look at our children and each other, and we wonder why and how some of us are smarter than others. We're not! We only think we are because some of us harness more of our own inner energies than others, therefore, giving us more confidence to channel the aptitude that lies within all of us.

Not anymore! Last week, Lasactka was released into the general public, latching onto the systems of each and every one of you this very minute. Within days, you will begin to feel your energies change.

You will begin to feel lighter and more capable of performing incredible tasks. With Lasactka, all your energy will be channeled to full potential. We will all be forced to use 100% of our intelligence, making us a society of great power, where we can overcome all dangers and build the greatest civilization known to mankind!" The crowd applauded and cheered as Samantha finished her speech.

"Thank you, Samantha. Let me be the first one to say, I truly admire your work. I have definitely felt a difference ever since Lasactka was..." Chris suddenly froze, his words slurring as his mouth drooped to one side.

His focus faded from his eyes as Samantha waved a hand in front of his face.

"Chris? Chris? Are you alright?" Samantha questioned, concerned.

"Duh... uh... what was I saying again?" Chris asked.

"You were saying how you felt different after Lasactka was released into the public," Samantha reminded him.

"Duh... yeah... oh yeah... I is good!" Chris exclaimed as he held his thumbs up.

"Chris! What is going on with you? Why are you acting strange?! I'm sorry, ladies and gentlemen, Chris seems to have had a concussion of some sort." Samantha turned toward the crowd and apologized.

She turned back to Chris and slapped him across the face.

"Chris! Snap out of it! What's going on with you!? Answer me!"

Without a thought, Chris doubled over in a fit of uncontrollable laughter. Samantha grabbed his shoulders, trying to pull him upright, but he continued to laugh and brushed her off.

Samantha stepped back, stumbling in her heels as she looked out into the crowd. Dozens of faces blankly stared back at her, mouths slightly ajar and comprehension gone from their expressions.

Their faces seemed slack, as if the muscles in them stopped moving all at once, and they began to mumble a strange combination of words and sounds. Samantha's hands shook as she backed away toward the curtain behind stage, head piercing from the overlapping murmurs.

"What?"

"Where am I?"

"This isn't home, is it?"

"Excuse me! Is this my house?" one of the women shouted to Samantha. "It doesn't look like it, but I could be wrong!"

"Excuse me! Do you know the password to unlock my phone!? I think it's my birthday, but I can't remember my birthday!" a man in the crowd asked those around him.

The crowd continued to become distorted and confused, trampling over each other as they all headed toward opposing doors in attempts to find the exit.

"What the hell is going on?" Samantha questioned to herself as she stared out into the confused crowd. "Why is everyone acting... well... stupid? Can it be? No, it can't be Lasactka. I perfected it. It's flawless. This can't be it! Can it?"

Fearful as to what she may have just started, Samantha kicked off her heels and scooped up the skirt of her dress. She then ran toward the back exit behind stage. No way could she escape through the front entrance; the swarms of people were tripping over and running into each other.

She needed to get home and out of the spotlight. Nobody could know she theoretically caused this. Nobody could ever know. She ran along the sidewalk, dodging and stumbling over people as she went.

The stones and pebbles on the asphalt were sharp against the soles of her feet as she made a last-minute decision at a fork in the road. She turned left toward her lab instead of going home. She had to find out what had gone wrong, why her virus had done the exact opposite of what it was designed to do.

Along the way, she began to see more chaos caused by the stupidity everyone around her seemed to possess.

"No! No! No!!! Not my car!" Samantha screamed as she watched two other cars collide into hers because the drivers had forgotten how to brake. "Fuck it. I'll run!"

As she continued to scurry, she heard people around her stopping arguments midway as they had forgotten what they were arguing about. She spotted other individuals drinking from puddles caused by the aftermath of the rain.

Samantha slowed and halted as a car screeched toward her, hopping the curb and crashing into a tree. Smoke billowed out from under the hood as a man opened the door and flung himself onto the ground. She watched, a hand over her mouth and tears in her eyes, as the man drank stagnant water from a puddle left over from last night's rain.

Automobiles continued to crash into each other along the streets. Startlingly, people inside climbed out as if nothing was wrong. Samantha's stomach twisted as she saw a man with a piece of bone sticking out from his left shin. Blood smeared across the sidewalk behind him as he dragged himself to a spilled garbage can. The man then plucked out a rotten apple core and began eating.

"No, no. This can't be happening!" Samantha whispered to herself as she picked up her pace.

Her lab was just at the end of the road. If she could make it there and find out what changed in her viral DNA, she may just be able to stop the virus in its tracks before it took greater hold.

Samantha's heart pounded quickly in her chest as she reached her lab and pulled out her keycard, quickly realizing that security had programmed the lock incorrectly, causing her to remain locked out.

After several swipes, the card still refused to read. Each red light mocked her as she was quickly running out of time.

You caused this. You are why these people are suffering. You do nothing but ruin everything, Samantha thought to herself as she continued to swipe.

"Come on! Come on!" Samantha repeated as she pulled on the glass doors.

Nothing. They refused to budge.

"Ugh, fuck this!"

She scanned around intently and quickly found what she needed, a large rock sitting off to one side of the door, purchased in an attempt to make the landscaping look attractive. Samantha picked up the rock and held a strong grip before swinging it as hard as she could at the doors.

The alarms shrieked as the glass shattered and spilled onto the ground. Samantha moved quickly, ignoring the way the shards bit into the heels of her feet. She needed to get to her notes. She needed to see what went wrong with Lasactka.

She raced down the hallway to her office, flicked on the light, and pushed over her bookshelf, tearing apart binder after binder until she found the one she was looking for. With the binder flipped open and fear instilling in her, Samantha traced the words with her finger.

"Fuck," she whispered, defeated, as her heart stopped.

Lasactka
The End of Human Intelligence

Chapter Three

The Creation of Lasactka

Year 2080

"All passengers, please be seated as we prepare for our arrival at Tenzing Hillary Airport in Lukla, Nepal. As always, remember to brace yourselves and hold on for your lives," the flight attendant announced.

Samantha Mare had taken some time off after graduation to climb to the summit of Mount Everest, her biggest goal since she was a child. She had always watched documentaries and looked up images on the Internet, in awe of the beautiful peak of the tallest mountain in the world.

She spent her past ten years training for this day and had been saving up for over a decade to pay for this experience. She couldn't remember the last time she went on vacation or even out for a drink with her friends.

She was ready. Nothing could stand in her way now as she neared close to her destiny. She could see the beautiful height of the mountain and already pictured herself climbing up.

"All passengers, please do not unbuckle your seatbelts. I repeat, please do not unbuckle your seatbelts. Passengers, please hold on tight and do not panic! I REPEAT, DO NOT PANIC AND DO NOT MOVE!"

Samantha's thoughts dissipated at the sound of a screaming flight attendant as she quickly realized what was happening.

The pilot had landed seconds too late at the world's shortest airport runway, rising at a height of over 9,000 feet in the air, the nose of the aircraft tipping over the edge of a tall cliff toward the ground far below.

Samantha was one of ten others on the small aircraft, all part of the tour she had signed up for to climb the mountain. Her heart was pounding as she looked out the tiny window beside her and saw the world around her rocking back and forth as the plane continued to dangle off the edge of the cliff.

"PASSENGERS! DO NOT PANIC!" the flight attendant screamed again.

But panicked they did, screaming their last words and prayers as they saw their entire lives flash before their eyes.

"Alright, passengers, listen closely. Everyone slowly unbuckle your seatbelts, and on the count of three, run toward the back of the aircraft. We are going to try to tip this plane back onto the runway. Ready, one... two... three... Go!"

With that, all the passengers bolted toward the back of the plane. However, their haphazard scurry only rocked the jet even more, and it eventually tipped off the edge of the runway and headed straight down.

Samantha closed her eyes as those around her continued to scream and cry. On her way down, she immediately regretted all the decisions she had ever made in her life that led her up to this moment.

"Why did I choose to go on this trek instead of staying home and finding a job?!" she cried to herself.

Samantha had just graduated from Highland University with a PhD in Neuroscience, specializing in human intelligence.

After seven years of diligence, she watched all her classmates go off to interviews and the start of their new careers while she decided to pack her bags and board a plane. However, during this moment, she lamented not having played it safe as she knew her life was coming to an end.

Crash!

"Several days have passed since the crash landing of flight 783 from Kathmandu to Lukla, Nepal. Ten passengers, two pilots, and one flight attendant all boarded the small aircraft early morning last Tuesday, plummeting over 9,000 feet into the ground due to a mishap in the pilot's landing flaw and so far, only a fraction of the bodies have been found. There were no survivors. More to come later tonight."

The sun began to set. The wind picked up against the mountains, and the temperature dropped. A piece of the broken wing from aircraft 783 began to rattle, struggling to budge as the thing below it attempted to push it off.

"Ugh," Samantha groaned as she looked around her environment after pushing the aircraft wing off her.

Her head spun and throbbed, and her chest ached with each new breath.

Maybe I would've been better off dead, she thought as she blinked rapidly and tried to get a bearing on her surroundings.

A dark blur passed quickly across her vision.

"Hello?" she screamed. "Is anyone there? Is everyone okay!? Is anyone alive?"

She continued to shout until she realized that she was potentially the only survivor left. Cold and lost, she wondered what she should do. She searched around for her bag, but it was nowhere in sight. The crash had caused parts of the destroyed plane to ricochet throughout the valleys and rivers of the mountains.

Hopeless, Samantha walked toward the direction that seemed the safest, toward the peaks. She had no money, no passport, no food, and part of her wished she died in the crash. For days on end, she trudged through the Himalayan mountains, fighting bright sunshine and snowstorms while trying to stay alive.

Since she had decided to embark on this trip during off-season, there was no one in sight for her to call for help. Three weeks passed, and she still found herself alone in the alps, sleeping in caves and keeping warm by building her own fire.

However, one day, everything changed. The cave she presumed was just another hole in the wall turned out to be the entrance leading to an underground tunnel.

"Hello!" Samantha yelled as she walked down a hollow tunnel, her voice echoing behind her. "Is anyone here?"

She walked further down the tunnel and soon came face to face with a wooden door that read, HYGOLTZ: DR. FARROW'S LAB.

Dr. Farrow? Samantha thought. *I know about him. He won the first Synapselligence Award in 2035 for his invention of a microchip that functioned as a brain independent of the body. However, shortly after he received his award, he disappeared from the face of the Earth and was never heard from again. Most suspected that he had somehow transferred his own brain into the chip and committed suicide as a result of it.*

"Who's knocking on my door!?" a faint cry came through from the other side.

"Hello? Dr. Farrow? My name is Samantha Mare. My plane crashed about 80 miles of here, and I'm lost with no food or money. Can I please borrow your phone so I can call for help?" Samantha pleaded.

Samantha walked into the lab after realizing the door was left unlocked and saw numerous yak brains in glass jars. Part startled, part horrified, she was fascinated to learn more.

"What is this?" she asked.

"Dear, I do not have a phone, but my assistant can help you wire wherever and whatever you need in the back," Dr. Farrow answered as if he did not hear her.

"Dr. Farrow, what is all this?" Samantha asked again, curious to learn more about these yak brains.

"These, my child, are yak brains," Dr. Farrow answered.

"What are they for?"

"People, ignorant folk, they all laugh at my work because they don't understand. For years, decades, I have spent my life creating the impossible, changing the world, and people laugh. People are too stupid to understand greatness. People are too dumb to understand life-changing inventions even if they slap them in their stupid faces."

"What are you creating this time? Yak brains. Ambitious."

"The Lasactka virus, guaranteed to make people less stupid, guaranteed to make people understand greatness, guaranteed to make people understand that the world is changing, making people realize that they need to keep up.

The Lasactka virus injects into the brains of individuals and increases their intelligence as quickly as you can blink your eye. People are not stupid because they are genetically stupid; people are stupid because they are genetically lazy. Lasactka gives people the knowledge without the work."

"Wow, that's really incredible. If you can get this virus to attach, it'll change humanity forever. I worked on creating a virus during my grad school years, a virus that could potentially repair dyslexia. Unfortunately, I was never able to figure out the right host to extract it from."

"You, you a scientist?"

"I received my PhD in neuroscience a few months back. Before that, I was working as an assistant scientist in a laboratory that specialized in early-onset dementia."

"You, you be my protégé. It is very difficult working here in the mountains. Nobody comes. Nobody helps me. I'm too old to keep running around. You help me develop virus."

Despite being desperate to go home and forget this nightmare of a trip ever happened, Samantha was also curious to see more of Dr. Farrow's virus. This could hypothetically work. If he could successfully create this strain, society would be unstoppable. All the greatest minds merged into one can create a world capable of endless feats.

"Yes, I will stay," Samantha responded confidently.

Lasactka
The End of Human Intelligence

Chapter Four

The Apocalypse

Year 2086

"It has been 75 days since the deadly Himalayan Lasactka was unleashed into the world, creating mayhem, and modern technology and supplies are beginning to dwindle fast. Scientists are forgetting how to create vaccines. Technicians are forgetting how electricity and water systems operate, and leaders of large corporations are quickly being overrun by their chaotic juvenile workers! We are seeing more and more people die by the hour, and there is no one left intelligent enough to stop this pandemic!"

The cold air bites into Miles's skin. It is a lonely and quiet night, but his heart pounds noisily with every swerve he makes. His eyes and ears are on the lookout for "the infected." A stray branch, which hangs from a tree, drops beside his car, and his heart skips a bit in surprise. There is no time to take chances now; the infected may be hiding anywhere.

"It's just a stupid branch," he mutters and drives on.

The apocalypse has been escalating steadily for months now, leading to a full demise of the nation within a matter of weeks. Most people knew the situation was horrific, but many remained in full denial that it would not fall to total destruction of societal structures.

The street in his peripheral vision is completely deserted. He can see smoke arising from the distance. The deafening sound of police and fire truck sirens that had dominated the previous nights have finally abated. The authorities are probably all infected now too, leaving no one left to maintain order.

For him, constantly being on the move means constantly surviving; if he stays in a place for too long, the infected can smell him out and, in a best-case scenario, turn him into an infected. Although his backpack is filled with knives, guns, and other weapons, he knows he is dead meat if he ever gets overpowered by a group of the infected so, the best he can do is to keep avoiding them.

However, this mayhem did not start out like this. He was not always on the run. The world was not always facing an apocalypse, until few weeks ago, when a deadly Himalayan virus was unleashed into human society.

Miles Silver doesn't know the complete backstory to the virus, but he had heard rumors about its creator before he went on the move. Whoever created this invisible force of lethalness had intended for it to spike human intelligence, enhance the greater good of the society, and increase the knowledge of everyone without the effort of having to lift a finger. But it backfired colossally; it went straight for the cerebrum of humans and degenerated them, turning them into zombies and imbeciles.

Lasactka
The End of Human Intelligence

Reasoning and logic no longer existed as fights broke out throughout the country. There were more accidents as people were no longer aware of the consequences of their actions, and morality had become just another word in the dictionary. Humans now yearned for each other's flesh and blood. Human rot lay wasted on the streets. Those who were not infected by the virus died of hunger as food was no longer being produced or transported.

Within five weeks, country after country went down in disarray as civilians stabbed each other, razed cars and buildings to the ground. There were no leaders left to uphold law and order.

Modern technology had never seen anything like it. Scientists could not bar themselves from the virus long enough to study and create vaccines. They were turned into victims before they even saw it coming, popularly known as "the infected." Plenty of people died by the hour, and there was no one intelligent enough to stop the pandemic.

Except for Miles, but it was too late. The world has passed its redemption stage, and the only thing left for Miles was to run. It took a long time for Miles to get used to the new modus operandi of things; he had hoped that the new order of society was just a temporary fad, and life would soon turn back to normal. Boy, was he wrong.

However, when the virus infected and took over the lives of his parents, his friends, his neighbors (the nice, elderly lady next door and the petulant old man in the complex below him who always pounded at his ceiling whenever he turned the music above silent), and even the charming waitress who always seemed eager and excited to take his order, it was as sure as dawn that the virus had come to stay.

He struggled to pull himself away from his current life, loving every moment of it, from the memories to the experiences to the joys, and he didn't want to leave them all behind.

Lasactka
The End of Human Intelligence

So, as he perused his luxury condo, adorned with navy blue walls and gold-plated paperweights, he looked at his belongings (which were all of high value and very sentimental to him) for the final time before he embarked on his journey. He knew there was nothing he could do to save the world. Humanity had so much potential. Now it's all going to be over. There was nothing left for him to do but walk away.

Only thing left to save was himself, and that was what he did. Even if he was infected, the symptoms didn't set in, not yet anyway. Before he becomes incapable of thinking clearly, he needed to get to the bomb shelter he found in the isolated nowhere while traveling through the bleak winter of Siberia. That was his only way to survive.

***

He remembers the last conversation he had with a human, a proper one. Miles just resumed work after a sabbatical, unaware and ignorant of the turmoil the virus had caused and was excited to reunite with his colleagues once again.

The sight he was met with was a horrendous one, not the celebratory party he had expected. His boss, who used to be prim and proper, was almost stark naked and feasting on what seemed like the body of one of his colleagues. Everyone had the same characteristics; all mumbling nonsense, all feasting on dead human bodies like they were zombies. It was a scary sight to behold. He tried to talk to one of them, hoping they remembered him enough to spare him his life.

"Run!" he heard one of the people on the office grounds scream.

"Sorry, what? These are my colleagues; I can't leave them like this. I have to talk to them and bring them to their senses," Miles shouted back.

"They're not your colleagues, not anymore. They're different people now; they have been infected by the virus, their brains all changing. They can no longer tell the difference between friend or foe. Once they get to you, you're done for."

Miles took a glance over at the guy speaking to him. He was like them too, but slightly less naked and still somewhat humane. He didn't get it. It didn't make any sense.

"How...how come you're not like them? You're infected, aren't you? Shouldn't you be trying to eat me?"

"The virus has not multiplied in my brain yet, but you better get the fuck out of here before it does!"

At once, Miles felt sorrow for the guy. Here he was trying to help him when he didn't have to. Miles knew he had to extend an offer in return, despite his desire for a solitary life.

"Let me help you. You see, I have a camp in..."

"Don't even bother; the symptoms will soon catch up with me. It is only a matter of time. I can't be saved. Just run! Your life depends on it," the man replied, cutting him short.

And so, Miles did. He ran as if he would never run again. He was terrified to see what the world had become.

However, before he reached his condo, he took a detour at his favorite stall to top up his groceries, preparing for his long expedition to Siberia. What he saw there still shocks him to this day: everything cleared off and burnt down. Only rubbles were left of the spoil. He didn't even see the owner, Mr. Munch, who was usually always there. Bright and early to greet his customers.

It felt like one of those heists he watched when he was a young teenager. It was so unreal that the same thing was now happening in real life. The streets were also decorated with roasted car shells and blown-up corpses, as entrails hung from streetlights like festive streamers. Truly, the world had gone mad.

***

A sight cuts into his train of thought. Peering out a few meters away, his greatest fear comes charging at him: the infected. They stagger toward him in zombie-fashion, hunger written over their faces. There appearances are too unsettling to even begin to describe. Their faces wretched, enough to make Miles vomit.

Over on his left, he sees some of the infected roaming, inspecting each sign, car, and piece of trash they pass as if they had never seen such strange objects. One of them begins picking away at his fingers, peeling off skin until blood drips rapidly onto the ground.

A few others appear lost as they awkwardly run into each other, yelling out nonsensical opinions. That is what the virus does.

Although the horde consists of children and adults alike, they are not human, not anymore. Dribble and pus fall from various sides of their bodies as they trudge forward. Miles is caught in a conundrum.

To go back is to return to where he came from, which was dangerous enough, and to go forward, where the infected is coming from, is to risk getting bitten or killed. But one thing is sure: this horde is all that's left around here. He could crush them with his tires, or he could...

SNAP!

One of the infected bangs heavily at his window. There is no time to think; he has to take action, now! He reverses with a force that leaves one of the infected flailing on the ground. He surprises them and can't wait to release more from his bag of adrenaline.

He abruptly swerves left, and one of the infected who has been trailing him smashes against the rear of his Sedan. Another comes at him bearing weapons; for that, he turns his car in the direction of the monster, colliding with him destructively. A blunt thud can be heard as the "thing" hits the passenger door of Miles's car and drops to the ground. Miles wipes his sweat off his brows, and a dark spot forms under his arms.

When will this madness end? He turns on his wipers; blood streaks across the windshield like drops of rain.

Another one of the infected almost catches him off-guard, a maniac on a motorcycle following him with a rifle. He would have nailed him too if Miles hadn't noticed the lone figure through his rearview mirror. Hoping to startle him, he slams on his brakes, and the maniac smashes against the car, the rifle flying out of his hands.

Miles then abruptly turns left, and suddenly, everything becomes quiet again while he cruises down a deserted alleyway.

This is so strange, Miles thinks to himself.

Just a few weeks ago, the infected were high and mighty; they were respected people in the society. Now, they are part of a plague, primitively murdering each other with rocks, and eating their peers and neighbors like zombies.

Even though the world is dealing with a nuclear doom, it doesn't mean the layers of humankind have peeled off. It doesn't mean the ability to think and reason have already faded. How could humankind have eroded so quickly? Had the layer of civilization really been that thin?

Society had clearly broken down even before anything really happened. Was intelligence just a mask for people's guilty pleasures, using this outbreak as an excuse to enact on them?

All is clear now, or so he hopes. He had killed all the infected he encountered.

As he cruises onto a clear road with a small backpack filled with little food supply, he prays to the gods that he doesn't encounter any of the infected before arriving at his camp.

Lasactka
The End of Human Intelligence

Chapter Five

Escape Toward Tragedy

Finally reaching the end of the road, fifty short miles from where he needs to be, Miles pulls over his car and begins to walk toward his camp, hoping he won't be murdered or eaten along the way. Everything around him is other-worldly quiet, not like he had expected anyone to be around.

They are all either already gone or had become too swine-like to even think of escaping the chaos.

He has gotten to the end of the road; the rest needs to be reached by foot. He steps out of his car, locks it, and put the keys in his back pocket. He quietly moves, careful to not attract attention. He anxiously looks around for more of the infected, but none are to be seen.

Although he does not expect anyone to be around, the quiet is unbearable for him. At that moment, his phone decides to ring. He wasn't expecting anyone to be alive, much less call him on a day like this. He steels himself as he slowly checks his phone and wonders what bad news it will bring this time.

Alas, it is only his alarm. He forgot to switch it off since the last time he went into the office. He turns it off promptly and continues moving. With only a measly 10% left, he needs to preserve his battery in case of an emergency. He chuckles to himself. That idea sounded as dumb as hoping anyone is still alive. He keeps going, until he reaches his safe destination where he is sure to die alone in peace.

The wind is now freezing as Miles continues to walk, his teeth chattering in his skull.

Is this what it sounds like when the infected masticates on skeletons? Miles wonders as he sees a moving shadow on his right.

Startled, he glances up and sees a human corpse dangling upside down from a large oak tree, staring at him with eyes wide open and blood trickling from his mouth to his forehead, a grim smile forever frozen in death. Cold fear runs down Miles's spine. Shit.

There are thousands of other human corpses lined up in the same fashion: all hanging upside down and donning darkness, their hands crossed over their chests. The apocalypse has eradicated more people than he will ever know.

This begs the question about the foolproofness of society. Is society as solid as the Founding Fathers claimed? Can an external factor just dismantle the balance of the modern world and make it come crushing down like a deck of cards?

Despite the alarming sight, Miles keeps on walking. His heart races with fear, and his palms are coated with sweat.

However, he consoles himself with the fact that they are all dead and can do him no harm.

But that comfort suddenly vanishes as one of the dangling corpses opens her eyes. She unfolds her arms and begins to flail them at Miles as he walks under the row of dead. He spots a backpack beneath the tree and hopes it contains supplies he can use.

The tangled arms of the woman try to grab hold of Miles's locks as he leans over to snatch the bag, startling him and scaring him in the process. She also tries to grab part of his body, her decomposing hands grazing his left cheek instead. Miles cocks his gun and slowly lifts his head. As he aims to shoot, he freezes in his tracks as a familiar face greets him with a bloody smile.

"Wait, Sarah?" he asks the infected body, fully aware that she will not be able to reply.

"Die, incompetent human, Die!" Sarah, or the thing that resembled Sarah, growls as she tries to grab a patch of his hair.

Luckily, Miles is able to dodge her but still cannot stop staring. That "infected" over there is not Sarah; it is definitely some sort of monster that had consumed her.

There is a slight madness in her eyes that is close to hysteria. Her body is covered in bruises and wounds, blood dripping from her gouged eyes. A part of her left ear is missing, and her body looks close to crumbling. However, this lunacy is not unusual. Right before his most recent partner turned, she had also exuded hysteria.

He does not hesitate to shoot; he brings the gun to her face, and it explodes with a single click. Sarah crumbles into debris.

Several memories of Sarah flash through his mind. For a long time, while he was still a fitness freak, he used to pass by her every morning during his daily jogs, the once-beautiful park, adorned with a large pond, adorable ducks, and pretty roses, has now turned into a murky swamp: an aftermath of the apocalypse.

"Nice day, isn't it?" she would always say as Miles responded with affirmation.

They used to jog together, spanning a large breadth. Sometimes, they would take deep breaks and gulp down water from their bottles, finishing it and gasping for breath because of the speed at which they swallowed.

Other times, they went on short walks, conversing in between. Because of walks like these, Miles discovered that Sarah's last name was Letman, and at the age of 35, she was only able to conceive once before having a miscarriage.

She also had a husband, but they divorced after two years. She was a teacher at Brightside Elementary, and despite all the misfortunes she had endured in life, she always managed to greet others with a smile. Miles always listened intently, finding her experiences and stories fascinating. After several months, their relationship began to blossom, starting with a kiss that soon became more intimate, the affair that Miles always wanted.

Sarah, or whoever she is, is no longer the person who used to greet him with stimulating stories every morning. This is no longer the person who drove him to the emergency room when he scraped his knee during a cold winter run.

You see, the infected are still human. Roughly four months ago, a deadly virus was intentionally released from the Himalayan mountains known as "Lasactka."

This virus was intended to enhance the greater good of society, increasing the knowledge of everyone without the added effort. The creator of the virus, Mare, as they called her, had expected Lasactka to construct the greatest society known to man, accomplishing endless achievements and generating knowledge far beyond anyone could ever know.

However, unbeknownst to everyone, this virus eventually went awry, and shortly after it was released into the world, it dissolved into the cerebrums of the population and caused everyone to develop mental retardation.

Fights and accidents broke out as people were no longer aware of consequences and morality. Reasoning and logic no longer existed as riots broke out all over the country.

Within five short weeks, country after country combusted, civilians stabbing each other and lighting cars and buildings on fire. There were no leaders left to promote social order.

The people had forgotten how to manufacture food and generate power, leaving cities to rot in starvation and desolation. The entire world was either freezing over or burning down, and Miles was stuck in the middle of the two.

Silver was one of the last humans to become infected, or so he claimed. However, since symptoms set almost immediately, he knew he didn't have much time before he became completely incapable of even thinking clearly.

The only way for him to survive is if he makes his way to the bomb shelter in the isolated nowhere he had discovered months ago while traveling through the bleak winter of Siberia.

Scanning the remaining barren trees, Miles sees more of the diseased beginning to awake. Nervous that one of them might flail at him again, Miles quickly snatches up the backpack as if his life depended on it, shooting anyone and anything that moves.

What are these things? Are they really evil, or are they simply ignorant to social order? Do they no longer remember who they were or who they recognized after they are infected? Sarah sure didn't seem to notice him, or did she notice but attempted to kill him anyway?

Too many questions rush through his mind. He must remain concentrated on one goal and one goal only: to get out of here before anyone else tries to kill him.

Lasactka
The End of Human Intelligence

Chapter Six

Isolated and Alone

After many bleak days of trudging through snow and shooting anyone who stood in his path, Miles finally reaches his shelter, which remains untouched, just as he had left it.

There is no one else around, not like he expected there to be; the apocalypse has done its job of eliminating over half the planet.

At first glance, the camp seems empty, the shelter he preserved for himself. But on closer look, through the opening, there appears to be someone inside, in HIS camp. Fear grips Miles by the shirt; he has only been gone for a few weeks, and there is already a stranger in his shelter. The worst part, he isn't sure if the person inside is a living dead.

Summoning his courage, he gingerly walks into the camp, sighing in relief when he sees the man lying frozen still. He isn't sure how long the man has been dead for, but given the mottling of his skin, he had to have died over two weeks ago.

For several hours, Miles battles with what to do: he can either drag him out, or he can abandon camp and keep walking so the others don't come sniffing around. With his luck though, he'd probably end up freezing in the snow before seeing any shelter in sight.

Dragging the man out to fend for himself may seem like the obvious answer, but what if the body's still contaminated? What if he had been symptomatic right before he died, and the virus still lingers inside him? Touching the corpse would mean walking to his own death.

Weighing his options, he digs out some spare gloves from his backpack and slowly drags the dead man from his shelter, burning both his gloves and the body before heading back inside.

He pitches down his heavy bag, filled with a couple cans of cold beans, and kicks off his shoes. His feet had become irritated with callouses and blisters from the long distance.

He gathers some wood to create a blaze, melting snow over the flames to create water for a shower. He then devours three cans of cold beans and passes out in front of the open kindle.

As he tries to relax on his thin sheet, his leg hits something hard. At first thought, it seemed like an ordinary stone, but as he digs deeper, he pulls out a journal dating back over 200 years.

After reading several pages, Miles discovers that over two centuries ago, the world had been plagued with a similar virus, turning into an apocalypse and destroying all of humanity. Whoever wrote this journal must have traveled far and away to escape like Miles had.

Shock washes over Miles as he swipes through several pages with amazement. The owner of this journal was clearly an artist, the book filled with caricatures of zombies, people eating each other, no food, riots, and fights. There were also caricatures of the owner himself, explaining how he went from being a stout, short man to malnourished within months. Down to the cause, the effect and impact, they were all the same.

Miles doesn't need a brain to guess that the man had starved to death, like he soon will. History always repeats itself because society never learns. There is nothing to do with the book now anyways; the earth cannot be redeemed, and he is only waiting to die, peacefully.

Waking up in the middle of the night to a burnt-out flame and reoccurring nightmares of the infection, Miles lies on top of his blanket, trying to come to terms with reality. Every morning in this isolated shelter is starting to become the same: horrifying dreams with an even worse reality.

Every morning, he continues to force himself to get up even though there is no longer any reason to do so. What's the point? He has no motivation to do anything anymore, living included. There are no longer plans or goals to be sought after except to simply survive.

He once lived a daily routine, where he woke up around noon every morning, worked out, and ate a hearty breakfast before going off to work. Now, he sits in this dungeon and waits for either his death or his impending tragic transformation, unsure of which would be the worst way to go.

His days now consist of waking up, building a fire, and eating some beans before falling back asleep next to the flames. The wind becomes more brutal with each passing day, the clouds creating an overcast in the dark grey sky, serving as a constant reminder that catastrophe has befallen upon humanity.

Miles had wasted his entire life saving up for a luxurious home, only to end up living in one made of stone.

Unfortunately, money no longer means anything when there is nothing left for it to be spent on. He couldn't even bear to splurge on new boots that were free of holes because he wanted a mantle made of marble. As his toes begin to freeze in the frigid snow, he realizes how poor his choices had been.

I should have lived when I had the chance. Everyone told me to stop waiting until I'm old to begin living. Heck, now I won't even have the chance to become old.

Loneliness begins to set in during his endless days in the shelter. Miles craves for companionship, but there is no one left alive to grant him his wish. Apart from food, human touch is all he wants. If he doesn't go crazy from the spread of the virus, he may as well go crazy from the sequestration and isolation.

However, he has his doubts: what if someone comes to join him and ends up pilfering his food, leaving him high and dry, like those bumbling idiots out there? He had experience with people like that, and he refuses to let that happen again, especially in a pandemic where basic amenities are scarce. He is no fool. It only makes sense that his best chance of surviving, for at least a few more months, is to remain alone.

When he was still in the area chockfull of the infected, although it was unsafe, he got his well-needed companionship. People surrounded him, and he had no cause to complain. He wonders if the virus still lingers, ravaging its terror. He wonders if it's safe to go back home. Maybe he has become the sole survivor on Earth after all, and the virus had turned everyone into cannibals due to lack of food supplies. That certainly seems like a risk he does not want to take, the risk he refuses to take until it is necessary to do so.

On the flip side, he needs food. Miles has enough water, shelter, and firewood to survive the next few months, but his dwindling food supply remains a setback. He wishes he had stocked up on more before his journey, but his options were limited.

Even if this virus has a potential end, he might not make it until then to bask in its celebration. He will soon be known as the idiot who died in a Russian bomb shelter because he was too impatient to wait it out.

All he has achieved with this escape is a postponement of his death for a few more months and sheltered quarantine from all communication, leaving him in complete seclusion. At the start of all this, he had considered himself the lucky one, the one able to escape the chaos, but doubts are now beginning to creep in.

These lingering thoughts continue to wander through his mind as he scuffles his cold feet through the white and fluffy snow. He used to love coming here. Siberia is one of the most wonderful places in the world to escape from the woes of society. Now, it has become a death sentence.

As usual, he tries to determine where the grey sky ends and the equally grey snow begins. And per usual, he is not successful. The ubiquitous never-ending hue of greyness that surrounds him had set in a few weeks after the downfall of humanity, with the hefty temperature drop soon following.

This must be what a nuclear winter feels like. Miles had always heard rumors about it; never did he think he would experience it first-hand.

Angst soon creeps in while nerves rampage through his mind over the shortage of food. It is time to decide, risk contact with the infected humans or remain safe until the food supply is completely drained to the point where he cannot hold out another day.

His main trepidation, however, is that he cannot assume that first contact with the infected world would be successful and lead to replenished food stocks. In fact, it seems rather unlikely.

Nevertheless, common sense refuses to allow him to wait until he is almost starved before initiating a risk; that wouldn't leave enough time to find alternatives. Besides, the thought of seeing people again, despite them being diseased, feels almost too tempting.

With this, he gathers his almost empty bag, with enough room to store a new supply of food if he is lucky, puts out the flame, bundles up in his 12-year-old parka, and makes his way toward civilization.

Lasactka
The End of Human Intelligence

Chapter Seven

The Unexpected Encounter

It has been days on this long journey, and over forty dreadful miles later, Miles begins to encounter more than just mountains of snow and ice. Never in his life have barren trees and suspended bodies looked so attractive. Still, most of his surroundings continue to remain disgustingly grey.

The occluded mist clouds his perception, and the brisk strikes of wind brush through the strands of his hair. No way the world could possibly continue to remain this bleak; the nuclear winter would surely crush every last bit of hope humanity had remaining.

A few short ways later, Miles realizes he should have turned back when he had the chance. The existing world is no longer safe, and he stands a higher chance of survival back home in the solitude of his burrow.

However, the thought of encountering people and potential resources is just too enticing.

Maybe I'll run into a potential non-infected. Maybe I can learn more about whether the virus is dying, and maybe I can go back home. I need information. I need some sort of hope.

The closer Miles approaches civilization, the closer he holds his gun to his side as danger is just around the corner. The sky is becoming more and more opaque as he presses on, with haze filling the air, almost to the point where Miles is no longer able to see the decomposing bodies lying behind him.

Further down the road, he approaches a thick barren tree with maybe one or two crusted dead leaves still attached to it, this time, free of corpses. Crouching behind it, he scours for more of the budding diseased and a feasible town to invade before proceeding forward.

Nothing. Nothing, except for darkness. Nothing, except for an absence of all light and all civilization. Shit.

Fearful and still cautious of the evil lurking behind the fog, Miles continues walking until he reaches one of the towns. He approaches a hoard of vultures who had torn into his car, the same location he had left it, leaving him to fend for himself. So much for his plan.

Walking into the once-urban society feels like walking into a post-apocalyptic ghost town. People are colliding into each other as if they are toddlers, cackling and laughing when they tumble in supposed pain.

Miles feels like he had just walked into a preschool of full-grown adults who are forgetting how to accomplish the simplest of tasks. From what he can see, the virus is still causing mayhem. Worse, there is still no food. All the shops have been shut down; shops that were open were still open with reason, there was nothing left.

His stomach begins to rumble louder, and his pounding headache returns, reminding him of his imminent death if he doesn't find some food soon. Whatever glucose is still left in him is deteriorating by the second. The fear of dying evokes fear in Miles, causing him to move further into the city, hoping that, by a stroke of luck, he finds a pack of edibles.

Armed, he saunters deeper into the town, ransacking all the shops he sees. Nothing. Everything had either been stolen or eaten. He considers eating the mottled and rotten carcasses on the ground, but concludes that death by starvation beats death by infection any day. He bows his head in growing disappointment. If only he had paid more attention in the Scouts, he wouldn't need to rely on man-made products to survive.

Night draws near, and the hungry Miles starts to count the seconds to his demise. The owls hoot, as if in preparation for his death. He sits on the curb and reminisces on all the memories when he had thrown away food because of a single strand of hair. There is nothing much to do at this point. Wait for death and hope it comes with ease. When he becomes tired of reminiscing, he switches to tears. Draining his energy on tears means that when death does arrive, he won't be able to fight it.

He can only rest in the solace that he has made it this far, a soldier resting in peace. He had fought a good fight, and dying from starvation would only be another sign of the fallen and corrupt world. The signs of death are already upon him. He can feel his organs eating themselves.

"The time has arrived," he whispers to himself as he falls asleep.

***

The next morning, Miles is surprised to find himself still alive. A little further down the road, he finds a convenience store, demolished and destroyed, with infant-like adults eating tubes of paint and plaster. He walks up and down the aisles just to find all the food packages ripped into and consumed, all but one box of dried pasta. It's his. He needs it. He needs that box of pasta. Miles hadn't eaten carbs in months, and he begins salivating for even one piece.

However, as he begins inching toward it, a grown man rolls over on a beat-up skateboard and begins crunching on his box of pasta like they are potato chips.

Fuck. So much for stocking up, Miles deliberates, infuriated.

Walking a few more blocks down, Miles soon discovers the hell he had expected; the streets are all empty, all desolate, all abolished, with the next closest town 100 miles away.

Just about ready to surrender in despair on his search, he hears a faint cry from a distance: the sound of a woman's voice. She can't be that far away, but should he really risk it?

He already has a short supply of food as is, and he's struggling to desperately scavenge to find anything, even expired food, to keep him alive for a few more months.

Can he really risk bringing in another mouth to feed and shortening his own lifespan that much more?

Miles hears the faint cry sound again, sharper and slower than before.

"Can I really live with myself if I don't act like a decent human being here and save her? What a nightmare! If I save her, I die. If I leave, my conscience kills me anyway. Fuck it," Miles says to himself in defeat as he begins heading toward her direction, continuing to tread until the cry becomes louder and louder.

He eventually reaches the exact location where the voice was heard but sees no one in sight. Miles had expected hordes of the infected to surround some innocent woman, petting her like a porcelain doll, but to his surprise, he finds no one.

"Hello!?" he screams. "Is anyone out here?"

No reply.

"Hello!?" Miles screams again. "Is anyone out here?"

"I can't. I can't. I can't live like this anymore."

Miles hears a docile, but raspy, voice repeat from above his head. He looks up and sees a frail and brittle young woman standing on the ledge of a tall building.

"Hey!" Miles screams. "What are you doing?"

"It's all my fault. It's all my fault. I need to die. I deserve to die!" the voice continues to bellow down toward Miles's direction.

"Hey! It's not your fault. Please step down from the ledge. Let's talk! Come on down!"

"No! Everyone's dying, and it's all my fault."

The woman is clearly hysteric. There is no point in trying to talk any sense into her. She definitely isn't going to come down on her own. Still, Miles has to get her down one way or another. Too many people are dying, and he refuses to let another one die under his watch.

Waiting for just the right moment as she paces left and right on the ledge, Miles fears for the woman's life, as one misstep will cause her to come plummeting down. He slowly raises his gun, making sure to aim at just the right spot, pulls the trigger, and successfully makes the shot, shooting a tranquilizer straight into her neck.

To his demise, the woman does not fall onto the roof of the building as he had expected, instead, she quickly comes plunging down. Fuck.

Luckily, Miles is quick on his feet and catches her limp body right before she smashes into confetti on the concrete sidewalk. Part of him is delighted that she looks like she clearly had been starving. Insensitive, but there is no one left to judge him.

Without thinking, Miles finds great difficulty in trying to carry her back to his shelter, trudging through the thick snow, melted ice quickly seeping into his frayed shoes along the way. About halfway, he wonders how much easier it would be if he had just left her there to die.

For Miles, it is surprising to see another human who hasn't been infected. Does she have a food reserve somewhere? What about the infected? How had she been able to fend them off? She didn't seem like someone who would engage in fisticuffs, so the only other option would've been luck.

For having lived this long, he gave her huge accolades. This also brought about the question of how he would cope from now on. Trusting his own senses almost failed him this time. He had gone in search of food and almost died. He just needs to go back to his camp and eat all he has left while waiting for death to come once and for all. Even if this stranger does have a food reserve, he won't bother her. He won't try to cheat her of what's hers.

Suddenly, he hears a sound. He can sense that something inhumane and strange is coming their way. From the noise, they are not far. The sound grows louder and more intense.

Although the sky is pitch dark, Miles soon hears a hysterical scream that stops just as quickly as it started. Vulgar rampages of cheering soon follow. It dawns on him that there is nothing to be gained here. This place, this society he once called "home," is now a dangerous pit, and the only way out is to run.

Lasactka
The End of Human Intelligence

Chapter Eight

The Unforeseen Connection

Slapping through the bushes and breathing wildly, Miles continues running until he is out of breath. It is a hustle for survival. Run or die. Finally arriving back at his camp, with exploded blisters and scratches covering the soles of his feet, Miles places the frail woman on the asphalt ground of his shelter.

Distracted by his seemingly heroic act in saving her back in town, Miles just notices that the woman is adorned in a bedraggled collection of soaked rags. Everything is tattered, filthy, and difficult for Miles to tell what kind of garment her clothing had once been.

Miles is never good at socializing with others. He grew up without a family; his parents ran out on him when he was just a child and left him with nothing, not even memories. Because of this, he developed a lack of trust toward everyone around him, avoiding people for most of his life.

Whenever someone stood close to him, he developed a strong urge to quickly flee. But, it's not like Miles cannot function at all around other individuals. He is still able to behave relatively normally in the presence of fellow human beings; he just doesn't prefer it.

Interacting with women is even tougher for him. He knows, of course, that it is expected in order to form any kind of relationship with females. He likes sex, quite a lot at that, but he just doesn't like the rest, including the expectations, the commitments, the endless planning of a future, and constantly living a life where he needs to prove himself.

Sadly, those are all aspects of a relationship that most women find crucial and necessary. Fuck women.

As a result, Miles was able to effortlessly and bitterly disappoint every single woman he ever had a relationship with, even though he had never made any promises. On the contrary, as soon as Miles had learned the rules of the game, he warned every single one of them that he would never give into their demands.

Still, many continued to overlook his warnings, convinced they could convert him, but eventually gave up and left, calling Miles an asshole and a bigot.

Now, here he is, the guy unable to live with a woman, suddenly sharing the confined space of a bomb shelter in the middle of nowhere with one. Miles sighs and gently places her unconscious and trembling form onto a thin blanket.

Her body is skeleton-thin, and she has small injuries and large bruises almost everywhere on the face of her skin. Fortunately, she doesn't look like she is capable of any immediate danger to him, not yet anyway; in fact, Miles doubts she would even survive the night.

As he begins to walk away, he hears a faint sigh from behind him. Surprised, the woman flutters open her eyes briefly and smiles gently at him, whispering "thank you" before drifting back into sleep.

While she slumbers, Miles sits on the ground beside her, watching her sleep while thinking of revised ways to survive his new unforeseen situation, when she suddenly screams and jerks upward with forceful energy as if just awakening from a nightmare. She looks around with wide eyes, confused and disoriented.

Without speaking a single word, she focuses her gaze at Miles, frightened. She doesn't even know this guy's name, and suddenly, she's sitting in a room with him. Her face is jaunt, and from what he could see of her body, she looks near death due to increased starvation, almost like a zombie or some sort. He could barely handle sane women; this one petrifies him.

In attempts to soothe and comfort her, Miles places his hand on top of hers, surprising himself. He usually isn't into human contact, but it seems inhumane of him to not do so.

He watches her eyes wander around the room, stopping when they landed on him. She searches in his eyes, refusing to break contact and mesmerized with his features, leaving Miles feeling scrutinized and uncomfortable.

Rather than pulling out a sharp knife and stabbing him in the chest like Miles had feared, she simply smiles at him once again, weakly, before leaning back down onto her sheet and closing her eyes, tension eliminating from Miles's body.

***

The next morning, Miles finds himself kicking and cursing at what he had done as he leaves the shelter to confirm the safety of his location. How could he have been so foolish, saving a random girl during these hard times, a stranger nonetheless? On the other hand, he continues to excuse himself in how his guilt would've eradicated him otherwise if he had not saved her.

After spending the morning gathering firewood, Miles returns to the shelter to find the woman sitting upright on her blanket, awake and staring straight toward him. To say that situation is awkward would be a gross understatement.

The silence between them becomes brutal, with neither of them speaking a word for a painful stretch of time. He is afraid of saying anything that would trigger the possible murderer inside her while she is frightened he would try to tranquilize her again. Miles continues to stare, standing by the entrance for an awkwardly amount of time like an idiot and pretending not to know what to say when in truth, all he wants is for her to voluntarily leave.

I saved her life. What the hell am I supposed to do now? I can't make any fucking promises about the future. Hell, I don't even know if there is a future, Miles reflects in his mind while grinning at her like a sucker.

To break the silence, he hands her some bacteria-filled water he had dug up from the murky frozen ground, and she starts to drink, shockingly slowly, as Miles had expected her to wolf it down like an animal.

He could not help but continue to gawk at the woman as she downs her drink, suddenly finding her extremely attractive. Once he looked past her bruises and malnutrition, she became a sight to behold.

The long locks he had grabbed hold of to rescue her hung, scraggly and unkempt, down her bare back, revealing more cuts on her cheeks and forehead as she brushes her hair back.

She catches Miles gazing intently at her as she runs her fingers through her tangled hair, and their eyes lock, breaking when she giggles and turns her head away seconds later, leaving Miles feeling even more awkward.

I'm fine. I'm fine, right? I sure don't need a companion. My situation is stable for the next several months or so to come, or at least it was. I already saved her life. I owe her nothing. I did my duty.

My only goal now is to get rid of her as soon as possible. Hell, I would even be a gentleman and drop her off wherever she wants as soon as she is strong enough, Spain, Africa, Peru, it doesn't matter, as long as she doesn't stay here.

Everyone still alive at this point has their own problems. Surely, she would understand if I don't want to burden myself with hers. I had already done an irrationally valiant act by risking my life to rescue hers.

Yes, dropping her on some road with those "things" doesn't sound completely justifiable. I guess I could part with a few weeks of supplies so she could defend herself on the road, but no way would I halve my entire life expectancy by sharing more than that. No way, that is too much.

Shit, is she still watching me? Exactly how long have I been in thought? Time no longer means anything to me anymore. Life is just stagnant now, with each day exactly like the previous one.'

"Come to a conclusion?" the woman asks with a hoarse voice, breaking Miles's stream of thought.

Her fragile condition had made her voice sound scratchy and thin, but Miles is still amazed by her calmness. After all, this is life or death for her.

"Um...," he begins to speak. *How the hell do I tell someone whom I had rescued that I'm thinking of ditching her the first chance I get?*

"It's okay," she responds softly, almost as if she could read every thought inside his mind.

"What?" he responds ignorantly, pretending to feign innocence to his fatal thoughts

"Do whatever you need to do. It's okay. I'd be dead by now anyway without your help. To me, you can do no wrong despite what you decide. I'll always be grateful for you. You'll always be my hero."

Miles strains to understand her as her weak tone makes it a bit difficult to hear, but what he could hear, made him feel like shit. Her hero? That shouldn't change a thing though. He still needs to do what needs to be done. He stands up and turns around, ready to say something, anything to light up the dreadful situation.

However, upon opening his mouth, only silence is heard, mostly because he could not think of anything to say. Not like it matters anyway as her eyes had quickly closed, and she had fallen fast asleep, probably faking it to make things easier for him. Damn.

Hero. You'll always be my hero. She had said in that thin, hollow voice of hers.

Shit, he ruminates. *Heroes are resilient and strong, and they do heroic deeds for other people without a single selfish thought toward themselves. That's exactly what had not happened. Never did, never would.*

The more he thinks about it, the more Miles wonders if he had ever done anything for anyone but himself. Sure, he had cleaned the dishes when it was his turn on those rare occasions when he was in a relationship. If he truly is a hero, he would have saved Ms. Bauer from next door, an innocent old lady and probably the closest Miles had to a friend, but instead, he left her back home to live out her destined fate with the rest of the infected.

Pssh, hero, more like the opposite is what it is, he continues to ponder. *So why did I rescue this woman over all the rest, depriving those poor weirdly-dressed islanders of their, well, whatever they could have used her for, rather than using her as a distraction for my escape? And incidentally, draining me of my least-replaceable commodity, food, thus shortening my life?*

Why did I feel like I wouldn't be able to live with myself if I had left her there? I left Ms. Bauer, and I don't feel the slightest of guilt about that. Perhaps my fatal loneliness really did overtake my logic, and I saved her out of pure selfishness for companionship.

After his long internal dialogue, Miles concludes his "heroic act" was simply a rational, self-serving motive, not in the least chivalrous. He could live with that. Having settled his internal conundrum, he curls up in his corner of the room.

Just before falling asleep, a stray thought swiftly crosses his mind, *It really is rather nice to know that there's someone in the world who doesn't think you're an asshole, someone who might, someday, perhaps even admire you.*

Lasactka
The End of Human Intelligence

Chapter Nine

Interactions with the Stranger

The next morning sees Miles rising bright and early. That sounds normal enough, right? It's not. Waking up early has always been his Achilles Heel, and he would become infuriated and violent at anyone who tried to force him to do so.

With one eye still sealed shut, he stumbles over to his stash of supplies and opens a can of cold beans with his pocketknife. However, before Miles could dig in, he finds that he is being watched.

Damn, he thinks to himself. *I thought I was the only one awake.*

Not wanting to seem rude, even though he continues to stand there cumbersomely, about to pour some beans into his mouth, he turns toward her and begrudgingly asks if she would like any, secretly hoping she declines.

"I'll eat anything I can get my hands on. That's what you do when you've almost starved to death," she replies with hungry eyes.

"Oh, I see."

"You better hide what you have though. It will take all my willpower not to gulp everything you own down at once." She lightly jokes and chuckles, hoping to break the tension.

"I see. Just tell me how much you want, okay? No point in wasting supplies if we don't need to," Miles speaks with obvious resentment and mild displeasure toward this living being who needs his food for survival.

"Okay." She smiles after realizing the man in front of her isn't relishing in her humor. "You're really sweet, you know that?"

"I'm Miles, by the way."

Miles's paranoia begins to make him think her benevolent words are simply ploys to get him to let his guard down.

No way could he or would he ever let the words of someone, especially a woman, overtake his trusted instincts. He has survived long enough on his own; now is not the time to let go of what he knows.

"Sam."

"Nice to meet you. How are you?" Miles forcefully responds, fully knowing he sounds like an idiot by asking how she is under such harsh circumstances, but what else is he supposed to say during introductions?

He couldn't say "glad you're not dead, now get out" because that would be "uncivilized."

"So, why'd you try to kill yourself?" he asks to cover his word fart, catching himself too late for his insensitive question.

"It's my fault that everyone… you know what, just forget it. I don't really want to talk about that right now," Sam responds with an anemic smile.

Suddenly at a loss for words, she begins to cry, with no tears coming out. Miles can't seem to even begin imagining what had happened to her to cause her to almost commit suicide. Again, his thoughts are met with silence.

Sam quickly pulls herself together and looks him in the eyes again.

Here it comes, Miles dreadfully voices in his head. *She's going to say something that will make it impossible to get rid of her. I need her to go!*

"Thank you, Miles," she articulates.

"For what?"

"For saving me. I know that was a threatening decision for you."

She's right, and they both know it, so Miles remains inaudible. The bonding he had feared has already started. This being is no longer 110lbs of needy humanity; this human being is Sam, a living soul with a life and a name.

Still, Miles is determined not to deter from doing what needs to be done. His life depends on his self-discipline.

"Don't worry, Miles. Whatever you plan to do with me, it's still better than the fate you've rescued me from."

Damn, is she reading my mind or something? Does she know I'm trying to throw her as bait to those creatures out there?

Not knowing what to say that wouldn't potentially offend her again, Miles remains inelegantly still until he unexpectedly dozes off.

Several hours later, Miles wakes up, startled when he realizes Sam had been roaming around unsupervised while he snoozed. Clearly, he is still very alive, so maybe she isn't out to eradicate him after all.

He looks down at his torso and touches a soft blanket covering him that had not been there before he fell asleep.

"Sam," Miles whispers as he looks around the shelter and sees her nowhere in sight. "Maybe she left. Maybe she decided she was a burden and chose to take herself out of my equation."

Trying to hold back his presumed excitement, he pulls his parka over his shoulders and exits the shelter. To his unfortunate surprise, he sees Sam warming her cold hands over an open fire. She sees him and could almost predict the thoughts running through his mind as sweat travels down Miles's temple, despite the frozen tundra they are immersed in.

"You can trust me," Sam reassures Miles with a temperate smile as she sees panic wash over his face.

Not knowing why, Miles suddenly feels relaxed with Sam's presence. He never thought he could fully trust another human being as he never had before in his entire life, but Sam seems to be able to stir up positive and warm feelings inside him.

With her simple smile, well, and the fact that she didn't kill him in his sleep, Miles feels as if he can now depend his survival on her. His previous thought of wanting to drop her off and feed her to the cannibals begins to rattle a sense of guilt within him.

"Yeah, I know," he responds, both fully knowing the implications.

"Good," she smiles harmoniously.

Taking a closer look at her, Miles notices something different about her face. She looks so, well, beautiful. Then he realizes why. She is clean, and she looks incredible when she's not covered in dirt and filth. He could feel a tingling sensation running through him, a sensation that he had only ever felt when he was in lust.

Sam's transformation from a nameless and sexless entity to a real woman is enough to make Miles forget why he ever doubted her in the first place.

Despite months alone in isolation, he still feels no real romantic attraction toward her. Not yet, anyway.

However, Miles can already see that she is a very attractive woman, and it isn't difficult to predict the effect she would have on him once she regains her strength.

With this thought emerging in his mind, he needs to get rid of her quick if he decides he wants to do it; once she is back on her feet, she may become difficult to destroy, or even worse, he may end up developing feelings for his nemesis.

"I'm thinking maybe we can venture out in a few days and search for some supplies," she speaks as Miles continues to stare at her.

"Do you know of a place? The town where I found you was completely run dry," Miles questions in disbelief.

"Tannersville. You made the mistake of tackling the towns during the day. At night, the infected all fall asleep, leaving the supplies untouched. But I know a place, Tannersville, if you trust me."

"Sounds risky," Miles answers, fully knowing he would follow her regardless as his attraction toward her slowly becomes stronger and stronger.

"It's okay. I know you're worried, but we can do this. We just need a little luck. That's your strength, not mine."

"Okay," Miles responds, thinking this is the gutsiest woman, no person, he has ever met, much more fearless than he is.

Nothing else needs to be said. They sit quietly on a log, side by side, watching the grey and gentle clouds pass through the still sky, each lost in their own thoughts.
***

Hours later, Miles finds himself back in the comfort and safety of his city condo, lounging on his sofa with his feet up on the coffee table and enjoying a cold beer, when he experiences a sudden feeling of soft lips pressing against his.

He opens his eyes to find that it was all just a dream, and he is still stuck in this nightmare of an apocalypse.

Though, he would have been slightly more disappointed without Sam's smooth body lying on top of him.

Hey, I could live with this, he thinks to himself as her lips continue to glide along his. *A pretty good deal given the shitty situation.*

"Wow, not that I'm complaining, but what was that for?" Miles asks in ecstasy and thirst after Sam pulls away from him.

"That was... I don't know. Do I need a reason?" She smiles vulnerably at him, batting her extended eyelashes.

"No, no, certainly not. Feel free to keep going if you want some more." Miles grins, praying he doesn't appear moronic.

"That was for you being you," she cryptically says.

Women... Me being me? The unanimous opinion in the past had been that I was a douchebag. Either I had changed, or she is into kissing imbeciles.

His train of thought is interrupted rather rudely by another soulful kiss, this one with full lips and a massage of the tongue.

Damn, I could get used to this. I could get used to this if I don't fuck things up by kicking her out. No, I can't get used to this. The temptation would surely suck me in.

They stare into each other's eyes and can feel the stirring lust again. They grab each other in such frenzy, kissing and moaning in ecstasy. They certainly can't get enough. They thirst and crave for each other. His lips continue to glide into hers, thrusting and pulling. Other times, it follows with a full kiss and a massage of the tongue.

It has been a long time since each of them felt like this toward anyone, and it excited them. A silver lining in a shitty situation. It is the only novelty the evening brought, but neither of them complained. They try it several more times, almost too many times, and they both loved it.

As it grows darker, she snuggles in his arms, and together, they watch the featureless and depressing room as it reminds them of their impending doom. It doesn't matter, though. They are together and happy.

***

The following night seeks to be the first they spend together, truly together, doing absolutely nothing but snuggle and kiss. For some reason, her nightmares of her secret past don't seem to haunt her as much anymore as long as she remains snuggled by his side.

Nonetheless, Miles is willing to make that sacrifice for this noble endeavor. Strangely, his own, admittedly much milder, nightmares have stopped as well since she entered his life.

He had planned for such a disaster. He had money, and he used it to isolate himself as best he could from the effects of humanity's self-destruction. He had bravely gotten away, physically unscathed with supplies intact.

With all that though, if it hadn't been for Sam, Miles would still be wandering aimlessly around Siberia, counting the days until he runs out of food and dies.

Perhaps, in some subconscious way, he had chosen that way to die. Not for him to die in the brilliant light of a nuclear holocaust, or to find himself on the losing side in a mafia war and bleed out in a street somewhere.

No, he would survive the catastrophe with his own wits, preparation, and money, only to hide in the middle of Siberia until death found him, a passive victim. Typical Miles, despite all his money and selfishness, he still could not save himself.

Miles took one proactive step in salvaging Sam, a decision he had been regretting the past several days. Now, he is planning for a long-term future with her.

What has he become? Who has he become? That determined optimism of hers is contagious. Even more than that, she had given him a kick in the ass and a jump start into a whole different world he had been unknown to.

Lasactka
The End of Human Intelligence

Chapter Ten

In Search for Freedom

A few nights later, Sam and Miles find themselves trudging through thick snow toward Tannersville. Miles continues to shiver in the frigidity, with anxiety washing over him, while Sam remains calm.

He continues to wonder how she could remain so damn calm when they're both headed toward their terminations. Maybe having already survived hell had made her tougher, less worried about the future.

They remain uncommunicative as they approach the run-down town of Tannersville. She leads, as she knows the town much better than he does. There is no one to be seen anywhere.

Maybe she's right about the greatly decreased population density in Tannersville. Miles feels a great deal of sorrow and culpability for all who had died, but at that moment, he sees it as a saving grace as the competition for resources had been eliminated.

"It's that small building right over there," Sam points out as they approach the entrance of the town.

"Alright ba... I mean, Sam." Miles catches himself and smiles coyly to hide his embarrassment.

There is a time and place for romance, and this isn't it. He looks at her, and then it dawns on him that she hadn't noticed the costly mistake he just made. There is a fiery drive in her, a determination to accomplish their mission.

'Time to get shit done. Why not? Not like there's a whole lot waiting to get done today.' Miles reflects as he follows Sam's cautious steps around the bodies and traps.

Finally reaching the shop, Miles squints through the glass door to see if anyone is waiting for them inside. He couldn't see anyone, but that doesn't mean much; it's too dark to see even if there is a large crowd waiting inside. The shelves near the door appears to be mostly empty.

As expected, the shelves had already been torn down one by one by their predecessors in burglary. He looks around his surroundings several times before generating the nerve to enter the store.

But something feels wrong. Miles knows it, feels it. Someone is watching them. Miles begins to panic and looks back at Sam, who calmly alternates between checking her surroundings and trying to look inside the shop.

"Okay, you have the knife, and you're the man. Open the door and go in. I'll have your back with this stick," she finally speaks up with her own self-devised plan.

Did that sound like a plan? Fuck no! It sounded like suicide. We have no idea who or what is waiting inside this wretched place, and here she is telling me to go in first. Still, Sam is my woman now, and I'd have to protect her.

That's the moment Miles realizes he had never protected anybody or had been protected by anyone before. It didn't need to take a shitty situation for him to prove his love for her, but it needs to be done.

Wait, what? Love? Did I just think that? Anyway, time to open that damn door.

It creaks like a bitch even when he tries to open it silently. To his relief, nothing jumps out at him. He tentatively inches his way inside, his eyes blinding as they adjust to the dark and dust inside the store. He can hear noise coming from all directions around him but can't see a damn thing.

Cold fear courses through his body as he continues to stride with light steps. Just to do something, he takes out his knife and points in a random direction, stabbing air in attempts to impress Sam.

Like an idiot, he even makes some "huh" noises as a rat scuttles out of the door while Sam unsuccessfully tries to hide her nonstop giggling.

"Clearly, you were in some sort of special forces unit," Sam jokes from behind.

"Hey, don't mock me..." Miles tries to remain indignant before he starts to smile as well, his eyes adjusting to his surroundings as he searches around.

"Don't worry about it. I'll get what we need." Sam laughs a bit more, leaving Miles feeling weak and incapable.

Miles sees the shop littered with opened containers and small packages of rice. He grabs as many as he can hold and heads out the door.

"That's it. Let's get out of here, Sam."

They turn around to leave, realizing two things. One, they haven't checked their surroundings in a while and two, there is a burly man standing by the front door, nonchalantly watching them. He is wearing a blue bandana on his head, and Miles briefly wonders whether that is a gang symbol or just a terrible fashion statement.

The man is dressed in what might have been some kind of mechanic's overall during the medieval times, but is now just cloth hanging from him in a haphazard manner. He is clearly on the verge of starvation, looking so grey that Miles is afraid he would dissolve into dust at any moment. His panic finally turns into pity as he stares into the vacant, hollow eyes. This is a dead man walking.

Miles's pity evaporates as he slowly shakes his head as if to clear it. Frozen in place, Miles watches as the man closes in on them. There is dried blood mixed with rust along his dull blade. This would not be the man's first time. This man knows what he is doing. He begins to slowly wobble toward Miles, letting his outstretched arm and attached rusty knife lead the way. Time slows.

Miles has no idea what to do next. He doesn't have a clue about knife fights, already reaching the limit of his knowledge when he held his own knife by the wrong end. They stare into each other's eyes as the man continues to slowly progress toward Miles and Sam.

This unreal, but somehow frightening, scene quickly becomes rudely interrupted by the solid force of Sam's fist making blunt contact with the back of the man's skull.

The man tumbles to the ground surprisingly gracefully. Hearing his knife rattle on the floor takes Miles out of his stupor. He gives Sam a thumbs-up and tries to appear confident, like that had been his plan all along.

However, he isn't sure he had convinced her as she is busy picking up the rice and leaving the deteriorated store. Not wanting to be a total loser, Miles grabs two more bags and follows her.

As soon as they step out of the store, Miles is shocked to see nothing there as he had assumed more of the dead men would be outside awaiting them. But there are no gangs, no hungry hordes, no desperate individuals wanting to join or kill them. That guy had been alone.

Miles takes another look around and feels calm enough to take in the surroundings again. There are cars and buildings, what's left of them anyway, but the town is mostly deserted and abandoned. The grass and trees are all either dead or in the process of dying, a truly depressing site to behold.

"Coming?" Sam interrupts Miles's serenity, reminding him this is not the time to let his guard down as they need to quickly leave and head back to base camp.

Halfway home, Miles feels a light tap on his left shoulder. He turns around and sees Sam, expecting another kiss, but quickly realizes that she's pointing to the horde of about eight people heading toward them from a distance.

Although they are much slower, they are still closing in fast. Miles and Sam pick up the pace, but as Miles looks behind him, the horde is also doing the same. Shit. This is going to be a tight race.

Miles watches helplessly as one of those anti-human monstrosities inches closer and closer. Fortunately for Miles, the miscreation is greeted by Sam's outstretched arm, with a knife awaiting him at the end. His own inertia drives the knife into his chest, black sludge gushing out as he falls to the ground.

Sam had assumed a wide stance, but it still surprises Miles to see her remain standing. She has more strength than he had thought, much more than he ever would.

The fallen man looks up at Sam, confused, as if he had this one important question right at the tip of his tongue but can no longer remember what it was. He opens his mouth and points at her as if beginning a conversation, but all that comes out of his mouth is more sludge, leaving Sam still standing with her knife, towering the man as he clutches his chest and disintegrates.

Holy crap, that was impressive, Miles thinks as he gawks at the brute strength of his new girl.

She had just killed a guy, protecting the both of them, something Miles is not even sure he could have done.

While he is still admiring her determination and skill, it occurs to him that she really could easily kill him whenever she chooses. She has the toughness Miles lacks, toughness that could not be developed with money and pure solitude.

We did it. We risked a lot, but we also gained some, though not as much. Sure, we now have more food; that is a success that could not be denied. Life for us could have been even better if we were able to find some sort of protein to keep our strengths, but that hadn't happened. I guess Sam feels guilty for risking their lives just for some measly bags of rice, killing unnecessary humans just to survive.

The way I see it, if it hadn't been for her, I would surely be dead right now. However, the most important part of this trip isn't even the kills on our hands; it is the bond we created in the process. We are a real team now, Miles reflects on the moment they shared, fully trusting himself in Sam as their teamwork makes him almost euphoric.

Lasactka
The End of Human Intelligence

Chapter Eleven

Lasactka Creator Revealed

One luminous morning, while Sam is out enjoying the sun, Miles goes over to her blanket to fold the mess she had made.

I love her, but man, she is a slob, he thinks.

He picks up her thin wool blanket from the ground, and a small book falls out, almost like a journal. Miles knows he shouldn't read it, but he is too curious to put it down.

Maybe it's her diary. Maybe it's about him, her secret thoughts and feelings toward him. His curiosity overpowers his conscience, and he opens her supposed diary.

Surprisingly, in it are documentations, experiment-like writings dating back to over a decade ago. What the hell is this?

PROPERTY OF SAMANTHA MARE. DEDICATED PROTÉGÉ OF DR. JAMES FARROW.

Miles begins reading the extremely dense book filled with information on Lasactka, information unknown to public knowledge, dating back to when Samantha first helped isolate the virus from the brain of a yak.

The more he reads, the more he discovers that she is actually the creator of this deadly virus that wiped out humanity and human intelligence.

The Lasactka virus was supposed to save the human race by increasing their intelligence and giving them unlimited knowledge to accomplish anything. Instead, the virus had reversed the brain capacity of all humans to the size of a mere pea and turned everyone stupid and incompetent.

No. It can't be. Not my Sam, Miles ponders in disbelief.

He questions her when she returns from her morning walk and rather than denying it, she immediately breaks down into tears as she falls to the ground.

"I knew you wouldn't understand if I told you. That's why I wanted to kill myself that day we met. I had destroyed the world. It's all my fault. I should have stopped him. Dr. Farrow. I should have known all along that he didn't want this virus created to promote humanity; he wanted this virus created to get revenge on all those who had made fun of him for his elaborate inventions.

I should have known. I'm so stupid. I should have known better than to blindly listen to everything he told me. 'Just trust me,' he'd say when I questioned his procedures. But he kept reassuring me that he knew what he was doing so I just went along with it. He played me for a fool, used me as a scapegoat for taking responsibility of Lasactka while he fled, getting what he wanted but never having to own up to it.

I promoted this virus to people. I was so proud of what we had done that I stood by it. However, weeks after it was released, I saw people around me getting dumber and dumber. The city stopped functioning, and the world entered a mass homicide and suicide brigade. I'm sorry I didn't tell you. You would've kicked me out if I did," Sam continues to plead as her entire confession spills out.

She isn't wrong. If I hadn't gotten close to her, I would've murdered her on the spot for taking my life away from me. What the hell is wrong with this woman? How could she be a scientist, a doctor even, and not realize that she was releasing a deadly virus into the world? And to remain so proud of it? God, she is an idiot! Miles thinks to himself, becoming angrier with each word Sam speaks.

"You think I'm stupid, don't you?" Sam asks, her voice trembling.

Of course, I do! You fucking destroyed the world! Miles wants to scream, but instead, tries to remain still and collected. "No, you got screwed over. It wasn't necessarily your fault."

Miles could see tears beginning to flow down her eyes. Maybe she really isn't at fault for the demise of the world. After all, she had been tricked because she was just like the rest of the world, incompetent.

"Is there a cure? You created it. There has to be a cure, right?"

Still in tears, Sam looks up at Miles like a sad little puppy.

"I don't know. I don't know! I spent months trying to find one. I crossed every species I could possibly think of to combat the mutating virus strain, but each time I tried, the virus only grew stronger while the population of the people grew weaker.

When this virus was first released, it progressed slowly, making us think that it was actually benefiting mankind. However, the virus multiplied and mutated at an exponential rate, quickly spreading throughout the human brains and causing everyone to behave oblivious and uneducated."

"There has to be something you can do. Something! I had family who fell victim to this fucked-up bug. Do something!"

By this point, Miles no longer cares that Sam and him had something intimate. She clearly had given up hope and didn't seem to care about saving the world. Miles doesn't know if she was stupid before the virus or if she is just infected, but something must be done.

"This Dr. Farrow. You said it was his idea? His old fucked-up mind created this fucked-up thing? Where is he now?"

"I don't know. As soon as the virus was isolated, he just disappeared one day, leaving a note that said not to look for him."

"You don't have his number? Email? Address? Anything!?"

"I met Dr. Farrow in the middle of the Himalayan mountains. Everything he had was outdated. We were only able to communicate with each other because I lived in the mountains with him for over six years. After I found out the true purpose of Lasactka, I burned down his lab, fearful of what else would rise from it if I didn't."

"So, what now? You're just going to give up? Let all these people die from their own stupidity?"

"I don't have any other choice. It's too late!"

Miles now becomes very angry. He loved this woman, and it turns out that she's nothing but a heartless piece of shit.

Without saying another word, he grabs his bag, throws some cans of beans and a small bag of rice into it, and storms out the shelter.

He hates Sam, but he still has to leave some food behind for her; he refuses to stoop to her level. He could not become as heartless as her. His conscience would destroy him if he leaves her there to starve. At least she is warm and safe from the cold, unlike him. Miles has to brace himself for the frigid wind that awaits him behind those closed doors.

Lasactka
The End of Human Intelligence

Chapter Twelve

The Final Straw

Here he is, back out in the cold. It feels like it was just last week that he had walked through this same frigid cold to his shelter, the shelter that was supposed to be his saving grace but has now become his enemy.

What now? I can't stay out in the cold. The wind would send me to my death within days. I can't go back to my shelter. The sight of Sam makes me want to put my knife in her throat. There is only one thing left to do. I have to find this Dr. Farrow and get him to reverse this virus with whatever it takes.

But Miles has no lead. He doesn't even know the first name of this doctor or whether he's even still alive. The only information Sam had given him was that he has a laboratory in the heart of the Himalayas, or had, at least. Planes are no longer in service, for obvious reasons. Even if they are, Miles wouldn't feel safe getting on one as he'd die before the plane even reached the sky.

And with his car shredded into pieces and turned into a playground for retired lawyers, his only option is to walk to the Himalayan mountains. His feet are already frozen, and he doesn't know how much further his shoes would be able to take him.

Still, he has to try. He can keep telling himself that he needs to do this to save the world, but truth is, he is really just trying to go big to clear his conscience for sleeping with the enemy and leaving those back home to rot when he could have saved them. Even if Miles dies before he gets there, at least his conscience would be cleared.

Over the next few weeks, he continues to trudge through mountains of snow. Hell, Miles isn't even really sure if he's heading in the right direction. He has a tricked-out compass and a poor sense of direction. He figures he'd keep heading south until he sees some epic mountains.

Looking back, he regrets not paying attention in geography class. That way, he could at least get a sense of direction as to how far this place actually is. His best guess is a solid 100 miles. 100 miles. Shit. No way is he ever going to make that.

Miles clips his bag around his waist to secure it around his body. He then crunches on a handful of beans, now frozen as ice, psyching himself for the journey. With his estimate, he should be able to get there in under a week if he keeps a steady pace.

As he continues walking, the land that used to thrive with modern technology and prospering success has now turned to crumbling debris, and accomplished hopefuls have now turned to toddlers. It was just a short two months ago when Miles was offered the chance to become a part of Mensa.

Now, that society no longer means anything other than five letters on a piece of paper.

His entire life, he had worked diligently to get to where he is, intellectual, studious, and determined. Now, he's marching toward his death with no hopes of surviving his journey.

What was all that even for? What's the point of trying in the first place, wasting my life, if all that resulted is chaos and the downfall of society? It just goes to show that everything is indeed only temporary. I wish I had dedicated my life to learning more valuable and useful information, like how the bloody hell I'm going to get to the Himalayas rather than learning about the life of the Greek Gods. Thirty years. Thirty years I have wasted on useless knowledge. Thirty. Fucking. Years.

***

Approximately a week later, Miles finds himself still on barren grounds with views of mountains nowhere in sight. He continues trekking several more miles until he finds himself face to face with a sign: WELCOME TO VILYUYSK, RUSSIA.

Russia? No, no, no. It can't be. I should be a lot closer to Nepal by now. Not Russia. Miles looks down at his feet. Frostbite had claimed several of his toes in the frigid cold, and his skin begins to bleed from all the cracks and splits. *That's it. It's over. I can't continue. I can't continue my search for Dr. Farrow to try to end this nightmare. I can't save the world.*

Miles's legs buckle, and his feet turn numb with paralysis. He sees a desolate town in the near distance and proceeds to pull himself toward it, legs dragging behind him in the snow. This vibrant town used to be full of cheerful hopefuls and wise elders who have now turned into clueless zombies, colliding into cars and engaging in nonsensical conversations.

He ignores them and continues trailing. When the infection first started, he used to run away while blowing their faces off, hoping the infection didn't spread to him. But now, it no longer matters. He is already infected. He is already one of them. It is just a matter of time before he turns too.

Miles has no idea where he's walking or even going. He just feels the need to keep going even though he is fully aware he would never make it to his destination. Eventually, Miles's legs give out, and he collapses onto the ground, his forehead whacking against the concrete.

Out of the corner of his right eye, he spots one of the only buildings remaining in this town that has not been completely destroyed by the infected. Miles limps over and finds a metal sign that must have fallen off the front: PRYLER INTELLIGENCE.

He had heard of this company before. Long before Lasactka destroyed all intelligence and human brains, Pryler Intelligence was a social media corporation that helped people boost their online presence and status with their new app: Pry.

People had been so obsessed with increasing the credibility of their social media presence that their desperation had driven the motivation and creation of Pry.

Pryler Intelligence created an app that scanned the life of each person who signed up and completed a questionnaire of the life they wished they could live. Pry then created constructed images and captions that helped people showcase their "desired lives" and "best selves" without ever having to lift a single finger.

Pry offered people the opportunity to gain all the fame while doing none of the work. No longer did people have to ponder on the best words to say to capture the "perfect" moments. No longer did people have to perform endless research on how to beat out the competition.

With Pry, people were able to propel up the social media chain, showcasing their greatest wishes as reality while they actually did nothing.

Miles picks up the sign and tosses it onto the bleak street. Even a company like Pryler, one of the corporations in this world with the greatest inventions, had fallen victim to this virus.

Miles walks into the building through the half-detached doors and finds himself facing dozens upon dozens of smashed computers and whiteboards, adorned with a fucked-up game of Hangman. He tries switching on the light, but both the power and heat had been out for months. Great.

He continues roaming through the offices, where apps like "Pry" had been created, that have now all turned to storage for blanket forts.

"Well, at least it's better than nothing," he sighs as he takes shelter beneath one of the burlap-designed forts.

Miles reaches into his bag and pulls out Sam's journal. He was going to use this journal to jog Dr. Farrow's memory. It was more than likely that the doctor had forgotten exactly what went into making the virus. Miles cracks his bleeding knuckles. He would have been able to make the doctor remember, no matter what it took.

He gazes at his bleeding hands and the journal once more. None of it matters anymore. His hopes of making it to the laboratory have gone to dust. With all hopes lost, Miles flips open to a blank page and begins to write.

To those who find this, I'm sorry. I tried to stop it. I tried to stop Lasactka. I kept using the excuse of this trip as a way to relieve myself of the guilt, but I had so many chances to stop Lasactka from happening. I saw it coming.

I had predicted the impending end of the world sooner than it had actually happened, but I did nothing to stop it. I guess there's no need to hold in this secret any longer. I knew Samantha and Dr. Farrow.

I'm surprised she didn't recognize me, but I was on the plane with her in Lukla when it crashed. I thought I was the only survivor when I suddenly saw a weak girl push part of the aircraft wing off and stumble toward the mountains. I didn't know who she was or where she was going, but I followed her anyway, always maintaining a safe distance behind.

Sure, I could have helped her, but I didn't want to frighten her. I was there when she had the conversation with Dr. Farrow and when he introduced his concept of the Lasactka virus to her. I tried to remain discrete, but I foolishly tripped over a rock and fell flat on my face before them, causing them to notice me and pull me into their lab as their test subject.

I am patient zero.

I saw through months of trials, being forcibly injected several strains of viruses each time. After about three weeks into their experimentation, I was no longer able to think clearly. Then the final strain of Lasactka was ready.

They promised me that this virus would surely work. I didn't believe them. I knew there were going to be complications. I even laughed in their faces. But despite my thoughts, there was nothing I could have done.

They injected the virus into my temple, and my eyes began to blur. It almost felt like I was hallucinating as I faced a short period where I didn't even know where I was. I could have stopped them.

While I was tripped out, I overheard Dr. Farrow telling his assistant, Penlay, his true plans with the virus. If I hadn't been so high, I might have been able to remember to spread the word when I finally escaped... twelve months too late.

To this day, I don't know why Lasactka didn't turn me as quickly as it turned those around me when it went airborne. Perhaps the strain I was injected with was a milder form.

All I know is, I am infected, and I am destined to turn. I'm sorry everyone for destroying you. I'm sorry for being so stupid. I'm sorry for being so... oo... oo...

Miles suddenly becomes distracted and drops the pen and journal. He sees a torn electrical wire and walks toward it.

"Shiny... I need to touch. I need to touch now," he says as he inches closer toward the wire. "Fruity Twizzlers?"

With that, he grabs the wires, puts them in his mouth, and chews.

And everything turns dark.

Lasactka
The End of Human Intelligence

Lasactka
The End of Human Intelligence

We are all victims of modern society. We all want something more, something we know we can never achieve. And when we finally do, we perish to our own selfish ignorance.

Lasactka
The End of Human Intelligence

Lasactka
The End of Human Intelligence

Lasactka
The End of Human Intelligence

www.ingramcontent.com/pod-product-compliance
Lightning Source LLC
Chambersburg PA
CBHW032049180726
48284CB00004B/1251